# THE MINDSCAPE OF RUE BREAKERS

# The Mindscape of Rue Breakers

REUBEN MOSELEY

Urban Intellectual Books

# Contents

# Disability trumps all

I see all these people walking around,
Talking about race and colour with
So much rage.
Then I come through with
Something else to say.
And they all say,
"You're black so you know racism right?"
Well you'd normally be right,
But not this time cos,
You see people who are racist,
Are also dumb as an empty oil drum.
So disability trumps race,
In this rat race.
Cos you see people identify with what's the 'same'.
But if you change, well get ready to welcome hate.
So people tell me,
"You're black so you know racism?"
And I say nope
Cos I just see disability not racism.

You know people are dumb.
But the thing about disability is that it turns
Smart men to brain farts.
So people think they know jack,
Cos their friend Jack lost his leg
And has a peg.
Well I say wait a sec was he born this way?
Did he grow with sad eyes?
That all want to know why.
Cos they don't know,
And don't want to.
Be normal,
So they act formal.
But there's still
People assuming all,
Before they even try to beat me at pool.
With people thinking he's dumb,
On sight without seeing intelligence.
With having to prove basic intelligence
Just to sit in the development leagues.
With people seeing the legs without
Seeing eyes.
Without seeing,
The mind
Behind.
And when they do
They call you.
Steven,
Cos that's all they
Know.
All they know is Steven
So they think.

You either a blade of grass
Or as sharp as a hawking.
And all you want to do is say,
STOP TALKING,
Before punches get thrown.
And they have a wheelchair of their own.
So when a man says,
"You're black right, you know racism?"
I say nope,
Cos this curse,
Just hurts,
And trumps all.
So screw religion,
So screw colour,
So screw creed,
And belief.
Cos disability,
Breaks all.
And can't be fixed,
With sticks and metal.
And so people wonder,
Why for so many years,
Disability was hidden?
Cos it was hard,
As can be.
When the world,
Automatically,
Makes living,
A battle you have to win.
Screw disability.
It's a part of me,
But I choose whether it defines me

# Influences

All these kids
Growing up in the
World of Logan Paul
But now they're
growing up
Like fools with
50 DUIs
And blame it on the
Fibre wires
And wonder
Why the world tires
Then again these people
Be so dense
But then again that's what you call
Common sense
Nah fuck that
Just call it
Influence.
That's why a turtle's existence
Might be best
That part of the reason

I've got constant burn out
Then again
some people would
Rather be buried but
I'm not doing that
Cos I stay alive
Alone
But too hard on my bones
So I take it slow
And let the river of my
Mind flow
But still
Working on the performing part
Of performing arts
It's hard
But that's half the reason
Need some
Irrigation but
I think I got it
But it just seems
Like I'm picking up
More trash
Must look like
The thames by now
Still wondering
If half of my mind's
A clown
Am I still
A jack of all trades
Or if I'm still mentally
Sound
Or if my soul still

Bound
But it would seem
That I am still on
The merry go round
All these kids
Growing up in the
World of Logan Paul
But now they're going
To growing up with
50 DUIs
And blame it on the
Fibre wires
And wonder
Why the world don't care
But that's what you call
Influence.
Cancel culture
Call it cancer culture
Cos it spreads
And makes some feel
Like death and all their power
Left
But then some feel like
That's the only time
All the power returns to them
But it's just an exchange
And causes a thousand
People to die
And another lot to be
Greek demons
But they think they're Gods
But they're just like reef (A lost cause)

Shout out to da pharaohs
These days
My headlights be on
Snakes are easy to see
I'm more concerned about
Birds chirping.
In the sky
Why?
Cos the world don't get the
Social part of social media
You be looking for followers
Not fans
But that's just dopamine
So just dope I mean
Slave to numbers
Really?
You be looking needy
Seriously
Like someone needs
To get a matching set (snap you poor sap)
Just to survive that how I used to be
Now I'm past it
But not you
you're just out of it
Don't you get it man
You use snap and the book
So you can forget your troubles
Instead of tryna learn doubles
Still tryna prove you on the grind
Man why?
What you got to prove
You could be the goat it ain't hard

You got the skill and the dedication
But none of the vindication
All these kids
Growing up in the
World of Logan Paul
But now they're going
To grow up with
50 DUIs
And blame it on the
Fibre wires
And wonder
Why the world don't care
But that's what you call
Influence.
I know I use the bird
But call me illiterate
Cos the book
Be looking like
Nonsense
Still though
I try be on the
Fence
While speaking
French
Just cos of what
I just said
Some might wanna
Throw a wrench
But them just dense
I mean how many times have you heard
"I don't really mean to cause offence"
I mean fuck man

Like literally all these fools
Be schrodinger's douchebag
You be one thing here
Another there
I don't get the lie
You want to be a bigot
Like "men are strong and women weak"
How does that make a shit stick of sense
Then be your sad grey colours
And I'll be a goddamn rainbow
But you be like you picked that up from
Someone
Yeah my friends
My compass
That I made myself
But that's what you call
Influence.
All these kids
Growing up in the
World of Logan Paul
But now they're going
To grow up with
50 DUIs
And blame it on the
Fibre wires
And wonder
Why the world don't care
But that's what you call
Influence.
I look at the world
Get confused constantly
Overindulgence and over information

And I've had to bury my head in sand
Just to get some peace
And put my mind at ease
But all this stuff you call
Influence
All these kids
Growing up in the
World of Logan Paul
But now they're going
To grow up with
50 DUIs
And blame it on the
Fibre wires
And wonder
Why the world don't care
But that's what you call
Influence
And I call it
Madness

# Rue

Hi
It's been a while
I know we don't talk
I know you have all this pain
I know you look up at the sky
And wonder why
Did everyone die
I know You sometimes blame
Yourself
For the mistakes you make
Back in old days
When Danny had bare hair
And Mum was going off on shit
And you could still see dreams
I wonder what they think of us
And the mistake and opinions we've
Made
I know that over the years you gonna
Change
And some will say that's good
You'll have conflict

you'll create coping mechanisms
Like the twins
And some will tell you that your disability
Doesn't define you
You'll agree
Then you'll see
Monsters
And demons
You'll make the mistake
And you'll lose some shit
A couple of friends
And you'll be depressed
As can be
You'll hide shit cos self hate
Is a powerful thing
And this will slowly rip
You to sheards
Like you ate a bowl of lead
you'll be understanding grief and
Its infinite complexities
And you'll try to fight your
Demons cos dad didn't matter
Right?
But then you
Break apart
Cos of the stuff with mum
It'll poison you first
Slowly
You won't notice
You'll feel fine
But subconsciously

You'll lose your
Mind
Stop dreaming
Stop living
Stop thinking
But back to
2016
Dad dead
The Dursleys start
Turning into people
You'll worry
For mum
But you'll hold it
Inside
Till you break
Then you'll
Do it again
You'll
Start to miss
The old
Cos now
You're
Starting to feel
Cold
But its not even
2018
Mum worsing
The poison
Is doing its thing
You feel the distance
Like its covid
Inside you be feeling

Empty cos
You couldn't talk
Too many secrets
Shit you'll take to your
Grave or so you
Say
You'll realise that granny
Is bad but you'll
Hold hope
That we'll be normal
That independence
Is coming
But everything has
A price
And now mum's
Died
Your soul's
Cried
Half your mind
Died
You'll lose some more
Friends cos
They couldn't weather you reaching
The end of you teather
You'll grow close to the fam
But you'll be backing
Up 6ft for the safety
But then you realise
That your mum
Was a god you never
Saw
That social workers

Were worse than
You thought
You realise
As you get older
You'll lose that
Innocence
You'll want
To cry
But then you'll realise that
Your soul died
You'll realise
That, 6ft
Distance is more like
6 light years
You'll be looking
Back thinking
That 6 was light
Years
And 16 was deep
You had a hollowed
Out heart
But now you'll start
Rapping at school
You'll start
Writing poetry
To give your
Rage away
You'll scream and shout
You'll lose faith in everything
You'll begin to understand
Your mind
You start to fix the open

Wounds
But your pain
Will come for you
And you'll use the energy
Turn it into words
And breaths
You'll feel warm and fuzzy
With every scheme
And every rhyme
But then you leave
School with no good
Grades
You'll wish you were better
But you won't really care
Then you'll realise that everything
Doesn't click
So you'll go and see some
True MCs
You'll become
Better
You'll fight
For your
Chance to
Be in the best
Place ever
You'll see
Evil souls
But you'll
Start to master
The mind
Sarcasm becomes
Your weapon

Of choice
You'll start to look for
Peace
Now that you're armed
To the teeth
You'll find out someone
Feels the same way
At lust
You'll break it in a week
Cos demons be walking
In your circle
And you'll
Break your shell
You'll realise
That you're
So many
Beautiful
Things
You'll skip shit
Cos wandsworth
Wants you to
Question your
Self worth
But you'll get
God mode in
Rapping
During this time
And 2019 will close
You'll hope everything is
Good and you're right
Until Covid
Makes you livid

And you'll be stuck
In residence
You'll feel contained
Then you'll slowly
Start to change
Into an actual
Teenager
You'll learn
Performing art
And you'll become
Better
You'll start finding
Your style
Your mind starts to
Heal
But not the soul
You'll get
Happiness returning
You'll get to college
And you'll find new
Friends
And you'll be mature
And feel like the heat
You have inside
You don't deserve
But you'll care
you say
You're better
Right?
Acertory

# You made this dummy

I have been plotting
I have been planning
You are a piece of Shit
I can't do this anymore
Bye.
Everyone It's Aces
Back from wherever I go
With another rythme to send you paces
You see I got all this good energy
But as blacky says the energy you come in with
Is the energy you leave with
Please understand I came here feeling lost
But someone found me
So there's all this positivity around
And I don't feel like I'm in a dog pound
And for once I feel mentally sound
But I've been reflecting
Rethinking

Looking back at
The things I've done
And now I have I can
Let mercy wash away
I see the past
About when I
Had all the bad times
With Granny
The time I was
8 and she did some bad
Shit, Shit let's not talk about that
Or people are going to ask questions
Bless traditions
Fuck that shit
I get a glock
Then I lock it
Behind
The past is not present
So go bye
I see all the mistakes
But now I can see
The final take
And it's shit
But what can you do
I changed
I lost
I found
Something so bright
Something I can hold
Tight.
But you never saw

What I did to get here
The lessons I learned
The people I burned
And the names
I took to silence
The pain
The lengths
I've gone to stay sane
Are not for the faint
Of heart
But for me
It was necessary evil
It allowed me to
Find the ground and meaning
in all this
I finally know who I am
On this page
I don't need old men
Who talk in languages
Long dead
I don't need men talking in languages
So new that the old don't know
All I need is you
So I done a lot
A lot
Of looking
Of getting it wrong
If you think it was easy
Ima just say
It was like playing Sims on
Hardcore
But that's where

I found it
That pearl of infinite knowledge
Of my mind
I was looking
For a long
Time
Went looking in the past
Hoping I'll find it there
But In the future
That I found.
Was amazing
Full of love
And grounding
But I had to
Lose something
So important
I often
Question
Whether
It's all worth it.
Acertory.

# Tumbleweed

I am a broken soul
Lost my shit in 2018
This is just tumbleweed
I tumble and fumble
Break relationships
Like i'm Dumbldore
For some reason
When I rap I seem
To fight with my tooth and
Claw
I think its cos I like to go to
War
I just give my all
Even though I'm
A fool
I don't rap cos it cool
Or cos it'll let me ball
It's cos my mind died
And I like chaos
Like I'm part of
The tricker's bridge

Also rap let's me channel
My rage in to laser that
Kills all that cross
It
I don't spit fire
I shallow coals
Then create
Volcanos when
I rap
Just cos I'm bi
Don't meant
I'm a bitch
I just understand
My mind
More than you
That's what happens
When you lose
The manual to your
Mind and your creator
Flies in the sky
I look back
And I realise
That I didn't really
Have a childhood
When I went home
I saw death
But she kept herself
Invisible
So I could kinda
Function
Some people

Turn
To fighting all the
Butch bitches
Who'll come out as sissies
At 20
But not me
Then again
My body's a
Prison
Full of poison
8 year old me
Was when the cracks
Appeared
But how do you explain
Sexuality
How do you explain
Death
How do you explain
The mental gymnastics
That only you can see
To keep my mind
In one piece
To a kid
Who don't know what that
Shit means
You don't cos shit the size
Of a skyscraper
Is happening
And secrets are the code
We keep
I still sleep but don't dream
Wake feeling empty

So I fill it with lust
Then I dust off
And go through the motions
And wish for my demons to eat
Me while my angels keep saving me
Self preservation
Has no reservation
In saving me
I look at men and think
You never taught me shit
'Side from one soul
But he died
And I saw gods cry
And a little bit of my mind died
Then all this shitty stress
Starts eating me alive
My creator starts to break
But i'm willfully bind
So I can actually love
Life
Got to 14 my leash be strangling me
But really I don't want freedom
Shit be looking long
I just want to be like them
But I can never be
so I get to 17 and go to
South England finally
Leaving home
But by then I might aswell
Be alone
Cos my house ain't a home
It's just memories

Got demons tryna sneak
Up on me
Want me to trust
You
But you'd have to fly into my top tier
And you don't have the clearance
And no one sounds sincere
And so now my soul can't form
Being a husk is so much fun
No save states
Cos life ain't a game
Well if it is i want it to be
Fixed up like six second makeover
Cos this world is evil
And I'm starting to feel
And I don't want to
Want to be alone
Want to be on a throne
Though it requires dedication
But I'm a headbreaker
Look at me you
Why would you
You never do
It's too hard
To hard
To find me
Under all the fakes
Cos believe me
I don't exist
Cos God took
My soul and mind
Now there's just the

Tumbleweed
People wonder
Why I lost my
Faith it's cos
I lost part of
My soul
died
It's cos inside
Feels so cold
Its cos I trust
My darkness
More than
My light
So now I let the demons
Ransack my mind
Being a husk is awesome
My emotions
Can die
I don't need
To feel
I just need the evil
To seal
Away my awful ordeal
So I don't feel real

# You and I

I hate you fuck you. Well here goes
We've been doing this for a long time
We've been doing this, since the beginning of time.
Before I couldn't even count to five,
there was just you and I
In this war zone of mine.
All why wanna ask is why.
Cos I'm sick of you taking all my stuff away.
And just causing me pain,
then again you've kept me sane,
so now I want to turn a page
cos we're reaching a certain age
where things change.
And nothing stays the same.
Accept that you just cause me rage.
So now I'm switching lanes,
to a better plane.
With better aims,
where you complain and go away.
Cos I'm not letting you haunt me
like the bubonic plague.

Just You and I stuck in this loop till the end of time
Just you and I the leg breaker and jaw maker
Just you and I the hater and lover
Just you and I the fighter and the other
Just you and I the curse and the dead verse
You never left alone.
It's time for you to atone.
I'm not your home.
And I want to put you on death row.
I hate you. I wished you died. You're my flipside. My side
that can't fight.
But you hold me tight, you just cause me pain.
But without you I wouldn't be human being,
I wouldn't see all the things I'm seeing,
it's crazy you open my mind to what's inside cos you
change me hold me back from the
outside.
Unique to me there's nobody like you half the time I love
you and the others don't get you.
Not like I do.
Just You and I stuck in this loop till the end of time
Just you and I the leg breaker and jaw maker
Just you and I the hater and lover
Just you and I the fighter and the other
Just you and I the curse and the dead verse
But because of you people treat me different and start
to pivot
Start to treat me
Like I don't exist
Like I'm subhuman
Then again you've made me

more than human
you POS
I want you dead
But you're apart of me
So I can't server us
You're bonded to my dust
But I have broken you with
Blind lust
But it's not enough
And for that I hate you
Fuck you
You don't get it do you
Let me tell you
By the way
I hate you, I wish you died. But I have you till the end
of time
So you're mine

# About Urban Intellectual Books

Urban Intellectual Books is a publishing imprint
founded by black British indie writer Leke Apena in
2020. The imprint exclusively publishes books by male
and female black British writers across the UK.

Current books

A Prophet Who Loved Her
by Leke Apena

Flavours of Black
by Leke Apena

The Mindscape of Rue Breakers
by Reuben Moseley

Follow @urban_intellectual_books on Instagram
for the latest news on upcoming book releases